IN YOUR BED, SLEEPYHEAD

By
Melissa Saucier

Illustrated by
Stacy Hummel

For Kennedy Rae
You were worth every minute of every sleepless night.

I know you're feeling tired and
you want to get some rest.

But your bed is too crowded
for you to sleep your best.

Look! Here are some friends who are feeling tired, too.

They are filling up your bed, so we'll have to tell them "shoo"!

We'll send them off to some place where they'll get a pleasant snooze.
Time to listen closely and find out whose bed is whose!

The zebra wants to shut his eyes. It's time to go to bed.
Where should the sleepy zebra go to rest his stripey head?

He shouldn't sleep in your bed, so what should the poor guy do?

Zebras sleep standing up. They're comfy in a group.

The sloth wants to shut her eyes. It's time to go to bed.

Where should the tired sloth go to rest her weary head?

She shouldn't sleep in your bed. Where could her own bed be?

The sloth wants to get cozy up in a spacious tree.

The pig wants to shut his eyes. It's time to go to bed.

Where should the muddy pig go to rest his little head?

He shouldn't sleep in your bed. Have you seen any mud?

The pig should find a sty, and cuddle with his buds.

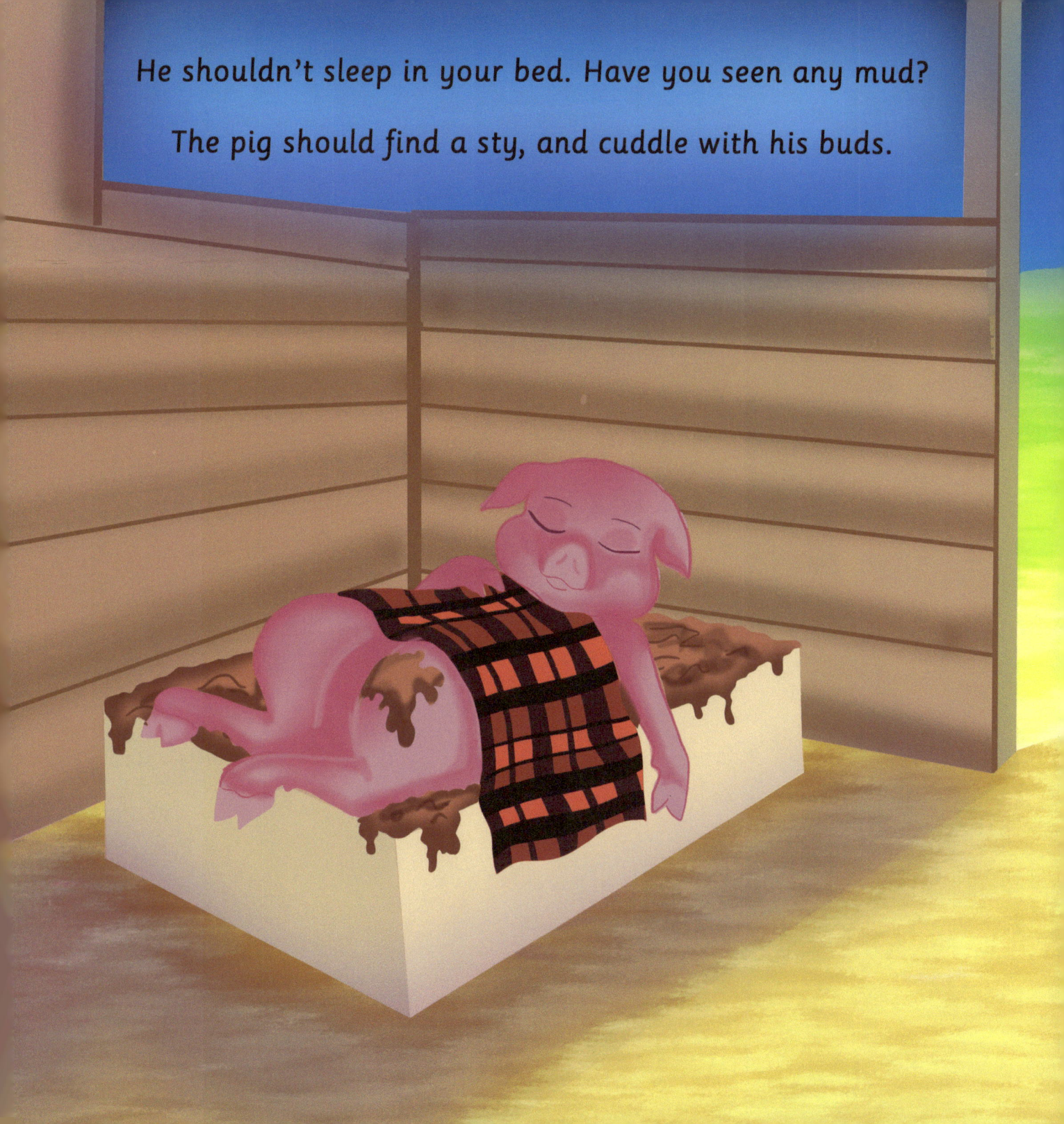

The penguin wants to shut his eyes. It's time to go to bed.

Where should the fluffy penguin go to rest his feathered head?

He shouldn't sleep in your bed. Where can he find some ice?

Penguins will lay right on top. To them, it feels so nice!

The cow wants to shut her eyes. It's time to go to bed.

Where should the big, brown cow go to rest her velvet head?

She shouldn't sleep in your bed. Perhaps instead a pile of hay?

This cow just might think that that's the perfect place to lay.

The owl wants to shut his eyes. It's time to go to bed.

Where should the howling owl go to rest his downy head?

He shouldn't sleep in your bed. Owls don't even sleep at night!

They like to doze during the day, when the sun is shining bright.

The bee wants to shut her eyes. It's time to go to bed.

Where should the buzzing bee go to rest her tiny head?

She shouldn't sleep in your bed. Bees need rest to survive.

The bee will make some honey and then rest in her hive!

The bear wants to shut his eyes. It's time to go to bed.

Where should the big, brown bear rest his furry head?

He shouldn't sleep in your bed. Should he find a big, dark cave?

Bears will rest in there all winter, and come out strong and brave.

The whale wants to shut his eyes. It's time to go to bed.

Where should the friendly whale go to rest his giant head?

He shouldn't sleep in your bed. Where could his big bed be?

A whale likes to sleep while roaming the salty sea.

The eagle wants to shut her eyes. It's time to go to bed.

Where should the soaring eagle go to rest her regal head?

She shouldn't sleep in your bed. Have you seen a comfy nest?

An eagle would fly right on in and take a nice, long rest.

It's time for you to sleep now. It's time to go to bed.

Where do you think that you should go to rest your tired head?

You should sleep in your own bed. I just know that you can!

Snuggling right on in there sounds like the perfect plan!

Pull the covers to your chin and
you'll be dreaming soon.

The shining stars upon your face,
beneath the bright white moon.

THE END

www.ingramcontent.com/pod-product-compliance
Lightning Source LLC
Chambersburg PA
CBHW041005170626
46815CB00002B/163